Africa II

Tales of

RETOLD TIMELESS CLASSICS

Perfection Learning®

Retold by Peg Hall

Editor: Paula J. Reece
Illustrator: Greg Hargreaves
Designer: Jan M. Michalson

For information, contact
Perfection Learning® Corporation
1000 North Second Avenue, P.O. Box 500
Logan, Iowa 51546-0500.
Phone: 800-831-4190 • Fax: 712-644-2392

PB ISBN-13: 978-0-7891-5068-4 ISBN-10: 0-7891-5068-9
RLB ISBN-13: 978-0-7807-9033-9 ISBN-10: 0-7807-9033-2
Printed in the U.S.A.

7 8 9 10 11 12 PP 13 12 11 10 09 08

Contents

The Woodcutter of Gura

AN ETHIOPIAN TALE

One day a man from the village of Gura went out with his ax. He wanted to get firewood for his house. But the trees nearby had all been cut down. So the man had to go a long way. He walked across the plain and down to the river.

At last the man reached a great, tall tree. He climbed up and sat on the biggest branch of all. Then he began to chop with his ax. But he was chopping the same branch he was sitting on!

While the man was working, a priest came along. He looked up into the tree and saw the woodcutter from Gura sitting there.

"Friend," said the priest. "What are you doing up there?"

"I am chopping wood for my fire," the man said. "What else could I be doing?"

"That's a bad way to chop wood," said the priest. He was worried about the man from Gura.

"It's the only way to chop wood," said the woodcutter. "You take your ax. Then you chop."

"Why don't you cut down the tree first?" asked the priest. "Right now you're sitting on the branch you're cutting. When you cut it off, it will fall to the ground. You will fall with it, my friend. You will be killed!"

"That's very silly," the man said. "When you want wood, you chop."

The priest shook his head and walked away. So the man from Gura chopped and chopped. While he chopped, he thought about how silly the priest was.

Suddenly the branch fell to the ground! And the man from Gura fell with it!

The man lay on the ground with the branch on his chest. As he lay there, he thought about what the priest had said.

"The priest told me that the branch would break," he said aloud. "He said I would fall and be killed. The branch did break—just the way he said it would. He knew what he was talking about. Yes, he did! So that must mean that I am dead. Yes, yes, I must be dead!"

Since he was dead, the woodcutter didn't get up off the ground. After all, dead men can't move. So he just lay there.

Soon some of his friends came along. They saw him lying under the branch. So they began to cry out. They shook the man. They talked to him and rubbed his head.

But the man didn't speak or move. He knew that he was dead.

At last his friends picked him up. They set him on his feet. But he fell down again. After all, dead men can't stand up!

At last his friends decided that the man really was dead. They picked him up to take him back to Gura.

"Don't forget my ax," said the woodcutter. So one of his friends went back to get it. Then they set out for the village. Along the way, they talked about the trouble that had come to their friend.

When they came to a fork in the road, they stopped. None of them knew which way to go. Some said they should walk beside the river. Others said they should go up over the hill. They stood and argued about it. And all the while the woodcutter lay across their backs. He lay still—just like a dead body.

At last the woodcutter could take it no longer. He put his head up and pointed to the hill. "That's the best way," he said. "That's the way I came."

Then he put his head down again and closed his eyes. His friends stopped talking. They carried him up over the hill. And all the while they talked. They talked of how sad they were about the woodcutter's death.

Soon they were over the hill. And sure enough, their village was on the other side. "He was right," the man's friends said. "The hill was the best way to go. He always was an honest man."

As they walked into the village, they passed the church. The village priests came out. They wanted to see what had happened. So the man's friends put him on the ground. Then everyone looked at him.

"We found him under an olive tree," one friend said. "A branch fell on him and killed him."

"That's not what happened," said the woodcutter. He opened his eyes just a minute to say this. "I was sitting on the branch, and it broke." Then he closed his eyes again.

The priests shook their heads sadly. Then the man's friends picked him up again. They carried him off to his house.

But when they got there, no one was home. So they put the man on the ground. Then they began to argue about what they should do. The poor fellows were so mixed-up!

After a while a dog came by. He went over to the woodcutter and licked his face.

"Take the dog away!" shouted the woodcutter. "This is no way to treat the dead!"

So the friends chased the dog away. Then they began to argue again.

The woodcutter got tired of this. So at last he sat up. He said, "Send for my wife! She is most likely down by the well. She will be talking to the other women."

Then he lay down again and closed his eyes. His friends did as he had said. They sent for his wife.

The man's wife came running to the house. She was crying because she had been told that her husband was dead. The other women of the village came running after her. Soon the house was full of people.

The man's friends told their story again. "A branch fell on him," they said. "It killed him."

"Oh!" cried the man. "I told you before, that's not what happened. I was sitting on the branch, and it broke. How many times do I have to say it?"

"Ah, yes, that's it," said his friends. "He was sitting on the branch, and it broke. He fell from the tree and was killed."

"He is talking," said the man's wife. "So how can he be dead?"

"It is sad. But you can see for yourself that he is dead," they answered.

"Maybe he isn't dead at all," said the wife.

Her words made the woodcutter angry. He sat up. "A priest came by while I was chopping the branch. He said I would fall and be killed. I fell. The priest was right about that. He spoke only the truth. So I must be dead."

"Maybe the priest was wrong," said the man's wife. "After all, he didn't see you when you fell. He only saw you before you fell."

"Argue, argue, argue!" cried the man. "Will it never end?" He got up from the ground. He picked up his ax and walked out of the house.

"Where are you going?" his wife called.

"To get some wood for your fire," the man said. Then he walked down the hill and out of sight.

"What a fine man!" the villagers said. "He is dead. But even at a time like this, he thinks of his wife. And he goes off to get what she needs."

Lion's Wings and Lion's Bones

A SOUTH AFRICAN TALE

You may think the Lion is frightening now. For he roars loudly and eats other animals. But you should have seen him in the old days. Back then Lion was big. And Lion was bad. And on top of that, Lion had wings.

Now, I'm not talking about little wings. Not bits of wings like Ostrich has. I'm talking about WINGS. Big wings. Heavy-duty wings. Wings fit for a lion. Not with feathers like a bird's wings. Instead, Lion's wings were made of bone, hair, and skin. They were like a bat's wings. But much bigger.

When Lion went off to hunt, no one was safe. He'd fly high in the sky. And he would look over his hunting ground. When he spotted a zebra, he'd pull in his wings. Then down he'd come. He'd drop from the sky like a rock. And when he landed, it was the end of the zebra! Even the impalas and the gazelles couldn't get away from Lion. When his shadow crossed the sun, even the elephants were afraid.

Now, Lion had one great fear. It had to do with the bones of the animals he killed. Lion was afraid that someone would break those bones. No one knew why Lion had this fear. But it made him a Cat of Great Care.

Lion would finish eating an animal he had caught. Then he would gather up every last bone. He would paw through the grass to be sure he hadn't missed one. Then he would close his jaws around the bones. He would carry them off to his den.

Lion's den—now there was a sight! It was one mean, awful place. Big bones and little bones. Old bones and fresh bones. Skulls, legs, and ribs filled every spot of the den. Who would be brave enough to go in there? Who would be crazy enough to do that? Even someone who wasn't afraid of bones wouldn't go in. No one would want to be there when Lion came back.

Even so, Lion didn't take any chances. He kept a pair of crows there as guards. Not just any crows, of course. These crows were pure white.

But Lion had more than two crows. In fact, every white crow ever born was sent to work for Lion. That's how Lion wanted it. So that's how it was.

And Lion's crows were different in another way. None of the other crows in the world could talk. But Lion's white crows could.

Lion kept all of the white crows together in a flock. He fed them so they would be strong. After all, crows don't live forever. After a time one of the guard crows would die. Then Lion would send the oldest crow in the flock to take the dead crow's place.

Yet even the oldest crow didn't know the whole story of the bones. You see, the bones held the magic that let Lion fly. As long as the bones were safe, Lion could stay in the sky.

That is why Lion was afraid. He feared that all of his plans wouldn't be enough. He was afraid that his guards wouldn't keep the bones safe.

And Lion was right to be afraid. For there was someone he should fear. It was Bullfrog.

Bullfrog! A mouth with no teeth. Eyes like those of a monkey. Hands with no claws. But

Bullfrog had a tongue. A tongue he knew how to use. And not just for catching flies.

One day Lion went away on a hunt. And Bullfrog came hopping up to the den.

"Hey, crows," Bullfrog said. "What are you doing here day after day?"

"Watching the bones for Lion," they said. "So move along, Bullfrog."

But Bullfrog just said, "Oh. Watching the bones. Tell me, are they doing anything interesting?"

"No," said the crows. "They just sit there."

"That's funny," said Bullfrog. "You sit, watching. The bones just sit. So it's hard to tell you apart. White bones. White crows. Nobody's moving except for the flies."

"Move along, Bullfrog. Move along," the crows said.

But Bullfrog said, "I'll tell you what. You can both take a break. I'll watch for a minute. Sitting is what a frog does best. I'll even take care of the flies for you."

The crows looked up into the sky. Lion was nowhere in sight.

"This is our chance," they told each other. "Bullfrog is right. With all this sitting, we are getting to be like the bones."

So off they flew. They spun and tumbled through the air.

The minute the crows were gone, Bullfrog went to work. He used his strong legs. One hop! Two hops! Three hops! A hundred hops!

High in the sky, the crows were flying. Down below, bones were breaking. Crack! went the skulls. Brack! went the leg bones. Crunch! Crunch! Crunch! went the little finger bones.

Then Bullfrog hopped away. He had only missed one bone. It was a tiny bone from a warthog's foot. Lion had hidden it in a far corner.

Soon the crows returned. At once they saw what Bullfrog had done. The crows went after him as fast as they could fly.

"Lion will bite off our heads!" the crows cried. "He'll use our bones to start a new pile!" They flew down to peck at Bullfrog.

Bullfrog took a great leap. He landed in the river. But the crows smacked into the mud.

Bullfrog called to the crows. "If Lion asks who broke his bones, tell him. Tell him to hunt for me here at the dam."

Then Bullfrog went underwater where it was safe. He said to himself, "Now we'll see what Lion does."

While all of this had been going on, Lion had been sitting. He was high up on a rock. He had been watching a herd of animals below him.

"Should I eat zebra today?" Lion asked himself. "Or giraffe? And gazelle is always nice. Still, zebra makes a real meal. They're fat and tender this time of year."

Lion didn't really like to eat giraffes. But a leopard had told him the young ones were good. "They take some getting used to," the leopard had said. "But I think you'd like them. They taste just like chicken."

"Chicken," thought Lion as he sat on his rock. "Do I like chicken? I can't remember. I think I'll have a zebra. No, a gazelle. Or maybe . . ."

Lion passed the time in this way. Meanwhile his dinner got closer and closer.

At last Lion was ready to move. But when he went to flap his wings, he could hardly lift them. He felt the power in them drain away. Like the water in a well that has gone dry.

Lion knew what it meant when his wings drooped. When they wouldn't hold him up. Lion thought about the bones. He let out a great roar. It was so loud, it shook the earth. The herd he'd been watching took off in fear.

Lion roared from the end of his tail to the tip of his nose. But it didn't do him a bit of good. Bullfrog had broken the magic bones. And the spell they held was broken too.

Lion had to crawl down off the rock. He had to walk all the long miles back to his den. And as he walked, he got madder and madder.

Meanwhile the pair of muddy crows waited at Lion's den. They ducked their heads in fear. They puffed up their feathers and cried. They kept looking up into the sky. They were sure that Lion would drop down onto their heads.

Then Lion walked up the trail. His tongue was hanging out. The crows were too surprised to be afraid.

"Bullfrog broke the bones!" they called out. "He said you could hunt for him down at the dam."

Lion didn't say a word. He just jumped at the crows. He was ready to bite off their heads.

Without thinking, the crows flew up. When they saw that Lion couldn't follow, they laughed. "We're safe!" they cried. "We're free as birds!" they called out happily. They flew back and forth over Lion's head.

Lion roared at them. "This is what I get for trusting crows! I feed them! I take care of them! And what thanks do I get?"

But the crows only laughed harder.

"Fine!" said Lion. "I'll show you!" And he dug up the one bone that Bullfrog had missed.

There was something the crows didn't know. The little bone from the warthog held the magic that let them talk. Lion snapped it between his teeth. And then the crows could only say, "Caw! Caw! Caw!"

After that, Lion took off his wings. They were of no use to him. He had to learn to catch animals on the ground.

And you can bet that Lion went looking for Bullfrog. But Bullfrog was very careful. He heard Lion coming. At once he jumped into the water and went to the bottom.

Lion sat on the bank and roared. But roaring doesn't solve a thing.

Circles spread out from where Bullfrog had jumped in. Seeing the circles made Lion even madder. They were like the circles he had once made while flying in the sky.

The Curious Monkey

AN ITURI TALE

Ah, let us go back a long time ago. A Dog was sleeping in the shade in the middle of the forest. He was all curled up in the ashes of a fire. And he was the first Dog ever in the world. It's hard to say if he was a Good Dog or a Bad Dog. Because back in those days, all a Dog did was sleep.

Well, that was fine. But then along came Monkey.

Monkey couldn't let anything be. He dropped from the tree to look at Dog. He looked from one side. Then from the other. He looked at Dog's head. And then at Dog's tail. Monkey hung upside down from a branch to see if Dog looked different that way. All he saw was upside-down Dog.

Monkey didn't know what Dog was. Remember, Dog was the first Dog in the world. So off went Monkey to tell the world. Monkeys just can't keep a secret.

All the animals came to see for themselves.

"Well," said Monkey. "There it is! Does anyone know what this is?"

Elephant leaned a long way over. She looked at Dog with elephant eyes. "No!" she said. She flapped her ears. "It's not an elephant. That's for sure."

"Not an elephant," said Monkey. "Thank you. That's a lot of help!"

Giraffe stepped up next. He swung his head back and forth. His giraffe eyes looked Dog over. "Sorry," said Giraffe. "Not a giraffe."

Sloth came next, taking his time. Some say Sloth is very wise. Others say he is only very slow.

Sloth looked with sloth eyes. But nobody heard what Sloth thought. After looking for a long time, Sloth climbed into a tree. Then he went to sleep.

Monkey called on every beast to come and look at Sleeping Dog. One by one, they looked. Each looked with its own eyes. But nobody said that Dog was one of theirs.

Oh, but Tortoise sat in a tree. And she knew all about Dog. She'd been in that tree since way,

way back. She knew just about everything.

"Done with asking?" she called down.

"This thing," Monkey said, pointing to Dog. "We still don't know what it is. And we still don't know what it does."

Tortoise answered in a calm, clear voice. "Until you think of a better name, call him Dog. He looks just like a Dog to me."

Oh! The sound of his name woke up Dog! And that made Dog mad! He opened his big dog eyes and looked at all the animals.

"Who woke me up?" asked Dog. "Never mind. I'll get you all!" And Dog ran at everyone. He barked and showed his big dog teeth.

Then Dog went after the animals. He had killing on his mind. All the animals ran away.

All but Tortoise. She just laughed and pulled her head into her shell. "You'll never get me, Dog," she said. "But from now on, you'll chase any animal your dog eyes see."

And that's how it still is. Even today.

That night, Monkey made up a new rhyme:
Now I
Know why
You let a sleeping dog lie.
By then, of course, it was too late.

The Rabbit Steals the Elephant's Dinner

A CENTRAL AFRICAN TALE

Kalulu the rabbit was watching the children play in the trees. They were the children of Soko the monkey.

He saw one monkey reach out his tail. He caught his little brother around the neck. The smaller monkey was held in midair.

Kalulu thought this was wonderful. He had no long tail of his own. But he could twist vines together to make a rope. And he could make a noose at one end of the rope.

For the next few days many animals were caught in this rope. They would twist and turn until they got away. They all thought they were trapped by accident. But it was Kalulu who caught them. He was trying out his noose.

At last Polo the elephant decided to make a new village. He was king of the animals. So he called every living thing in the forest to come. He wanted them to help him build the new village.

The only one who didn't go was Kalulu. He had smelled the delicious beans that Polo's wives were cooking. So he stayed behind. He waited until the beans were cool. Then he came out of the bushes and ate them up.

So when Polo got home, his dinner was gone. He was very angry. Who could have done such a thing?

The next day, Polo told Ntambo the lion to wait nearby. He told Ntambo to watch for the thief who had taken his dinner.

Now, Kalulu was hiding in the bushes. So he heard Polo's plan. He spent the night making vines into a big noose. He put the noose in the path near the cooking pots.

The next morning, the animals went to work on the new village. But not Kalulu. He walked out into the open. He started to eat

Polo's beans. And he watched the spot where the lion was hiding.

As soon as he was done eating, Kalulu ran off. Just as he expected, Ntambo jumped out and started chasing him.

Kalulu ran down the path and past the noose. When Ntambo followed, he was caught in the circle of rope. He twisted and wiggled until nighttime. Then the other animals came back to the old village. They set him loose.

Ntambo didn't want anyone to know what had happened. After all, he had been fooled by a little rabbit! So he said he didn't know who had done it.

The next day, Polo asked Mbo the buffalo to watch the beans. But Kalulu made a great noose. He hung it between two palm trees.

Once again Kalulu ate all the beans. And once again he ran off. The buffalo chased after him. But the rabbit led him between the trees. Mbo was caught in the noose.

All day long the buffalo twisted and turned in midair. At last night came. The other animals came back to the village. And they set Mbo free.

Mbo the buffalo wouldn't say how he had been fooled. He only said that there must be a trickster living among them.

The leopard, the lynx, the warthog, and the hunting dog were next. Each was fooled the same way. And every day Kalulu took Polo's beans and ate them.

At last Nkuvu the tortoise went to King Polo the elephant. Nkuvu was wiser than the rest of the animals. He said, "Have your wives cover me with salt. Then they can put me into the pot of beans. Tomorrow I will catch the thief."

So the next day Nkuvu was covered with salt. Then he hid in the pot of beans.

The worthless rabbit thought he would get another meal without having to work for it. The other animals left. And he set his noose once again. Then he walked up to the pot and began to eat.

Kalulu thought these beans tasted even better than usual. They were so delicious and salty. But before Kalulu could finish, Nkuvu bit his foot. He held on tightly to the little rabbit.

Kalulu screamed. He begged. He made promises. But Nkuvu didn't listen. He just held on to Kalulu's foot. And when all the animals returned, Kalulu was still there. He was caught in the pot of beans!

At once everyone saw who the thief was. They decided to pay him back. So for six days

Kalulu had to go without dinner. And when the others went off to work, they left Kalulu tied to a tree.

When the six days were over, Kalulu was very thin. So thin that the others felt sorry for him. They let him go.

But they warned Kalulu not to steal food anymore. From now on he had to work for it. They said that a thief may get away with stealing for a time. But he will always be caught in the end.

The Bachelors and the Python

A CENTRAL AFRICAN TALE

There were only two men in the village who were not married. All the others had found wives. But Kalemeleme was too gentle to stand up for himself. Or for anyone else. And Kinku was very bad-tempered. No one wanted to be with him for long.

So these two lived alone. And they were both unhappy.

Then one morning Kalemeleme grabbed his bow and arrows. He went off into the forest. There he shot two wildcats. One was gray. The other was brown.

On his way home Kalemeleme met Moma, the great rock python. Moma was the mightiest snake in the forest.

Kalemeleme was about to shout when Moma spoke to him. "Gentle one, have mercy on me. I am stiff and cold. Please take me to the river where it is warm."

Kalemeleme felt sorry for the snake. So he put the great python on his shoulders. He carried him to the stream and threw him in.

Moma lifted his head above the reeds. He called out, "Thank you, gentle one. I have seen how lonely you are. Throw in your two wildcats. Then take what the water spirit gives you."

Kalemeleme threw in the gray wildcat. Then he threw in the brown wildcat. At once the water began to ripple. It turned redder and redder. At last a great red mouth appeared. It was wide open.

Kalemeleme put his hand into the mouth. And he pulled out a gourd. He took it home and opened it. Out stepped the most beautiful girl he had ever seen. She was to be Kalemeleme's wife.

The girl wasn't just beautiful. She was as good as she was lovely. She could weave mats, braid baskets, and make pots. She kept the house clean and took care of the garden. She was a wonderful cook. And she helped the neighbors. Soon Kalemeleme and his wife were the most popular people in the village.

Kinku came to Kalemeleme one day. "Tell me," he said. "Where did you find your wife?"

"The water spirit gave her to me," Kalemeleme said. And then he told Kinku the story.

"Well, I want a wife too," said Kinku. So he took his bow and his arrows. He went off into the forest at midday. This is when the sun was high overhead.

Kinku killed a gray wildcat and a brown wildcat. On his way home he, too, met Moma. The mighty python was hiding under a bush to get out of the heat.

Kinku was about to shoot when Moma spoke to him. "Mercy, Kinku. Have mercy on me. I am dying in this heat. Please take me to the river where it is cool."

Now Kinku had never helped anyone but himself. So he said, "What! Help you, you terrible snake? Find your own way to the river!" Kinku shouted.

"Very well," said Moma. And he glided away through the bushes. Kinku followed him.

Moma slid into the water. Then he lifted his head above the reeds. "Kinku," he said. "I have seen how lonely you are. Throw in your gray wildcat and your brown wildcat. Then take what the water spirit gives you."

Kinku threw in the wildcats. At once the water began to ripple. It became redder and redder. Soon Kinku could see a huge open mouth just under the water. He put in his hand and pulled out a pumpkin.

Kinku headed for home with the pumpkin. With each step, it got heavier and heavier. At last he dropped it.

The pumpkin cracked. Out stepped the ugliest woman anyone had ever seen.

Before Kinku could move, the woman smacked him on the ears. Then she took him by the nose. "Come, Kinku," she said. "I am your wife."

She didn't give him time to say anything. She nagged at him and complained about him. She bullied him and blamed him for everything. And she was as lazy as she was ugly. All the time she yelled, "Kinku, get some water! Kinku, cut the firewood! Kinku, work in the garden! Kinku, cook the meal!"

Meanwhile she sat about and took it easy.

Of course, Kinku blamed the water spirit for his troubles. But he really had nobody to blame but himself.

Hare Causes Big Trouble

A SWAHILI TALE

Hippo and Rhino were once best friends. Each thought the other was strong and handsome. They drank from the same water hole. They even slept in the same mud hole.

Hare didn't like it that Hippo and Rhino were such good friends. Not when he didn't have a good friend of his own. So Hare talked about the two animals behind their backs. He said they were fat and greedy. He said they were loud and ugly.

But that was only behind their backs. If Hare saw Hippo and Rhino, things were different. Then he was all smiles. "Oh, you two are such good friends," he would say. "You are so good for each other."

Now it is true that Hare made fun of Hippo and Rhino. But he didn't really think they were fat and greedy. Or loud and ugly. No, he thought they were just the sort of friends he would like.

However, Hare didn't know how to make friends. He tried. But he just made the other animals mad.

He jumped on them when they were sleeping. He splashed in the water hole and made it too muddy to drink. All this made the other animals notice Hare. But it didn't make them want to be his friend.

Rhino and Hippo got tired of Hare's silly tricks. So the next time Hare hopped on Hippo's back, Rhino was ready. "Hippo, do you feel a flea?" he asked.

"It's a flea or a fly," said Hippo. Then he rolled over in the mud. Hare almost got crushed!

Hare didn't like that at all. And he didn't like being called names. For days he was mad at Hippo and Rhino.

Finally Hare made up his mind to do something. "Hippo and Rhino won't be my friends," he said. "So I won't let them be friends with each other!" At once he got to work on a plan.

First he made a long rope from vines. Then he went to the water hole. Rhino was there.

"Hippo said he's ten times stronger than you are," said Hare.

"He may be," said Rhino. And he laughed.

"He said you were ugly too," said Hare.

Rhino suddenly thought of something. Hippo had said something like that once. It had been many years ago. Long before they became good friends. His words made Rhino mad then. And they did now as well!

"Tell me what he said!" cried Rhino.

"Well, I don't know what Hippo was thinking," said Hare. "But he sent me here with this rope. He said something about pulling you out of your sorry water hole."

"My sorry water hole?" said Rhino. "Is that what he said? Well, tell him something from me. Tell him his mud hole is a pigsty. I would be helping him if I pulled him out of it. Tie your rope to my back leg. Tell Hippo to get ready to find another home!"

So Hare tied one end of the rope to Rhino's leg. Then he went looking for Hippo. He took the other end of the rope with him.

Hare found Hippo lying in his favorite mud hole. "Hippo," said Hare in a soft voice. "Rhino has been talking about you. He has been saying bad things. He says you are weak. And he says your mud hole is a pigsty."

"What's that you say?" asked Hippo. For Hippo couldn't hear very well.

Hare said the words again. Then he added something. "Rhino says he's tired of coming to visit your mud hole. And he says you're fat."

Hare held up the end of the rope. "Rhino wants to have a tug-of-war with you."

Hippo thought this was strange. After all, Rhino had been his friend for a long time. But then he remembered something that Rhino had once said. Something about how fat Hippo was.

Hippo felt pride well up in his huge body. He would show Rhino!

"Tie that rope to my leg!" he roared.

Hare quickly tied the rope to Hippo's back leg. "I'll tell you when to pull," he said. "And by the way, Rhino said you were ugly too."

Hippo got so mad! He knew he was more handsome than Rhino could ever be. He set off on his thick, short legs. Soon the rope was pulled tight.

At the other end of the rope, Rhino felt a tug. So he began to run the other way.

Hare sat on a small hill and watched. It made him laugh to see the two friends fighting each other.

Hippo pulled harder. "You think I'm fat, do you?" he roared. "I'll show you!"

Rhino dug his feet into the ground and pulled even harder. "You think I'm ugly, do you? I'll show you!"

Now the rope was only made of vines. So before long it snapped. And when it did, Hippo and Rhino both fell on their faces!

Hare laughed and laughed. He laughed so hard that he fell over. He rolled right down the hill. He rolled past Rhino, who started to run after him. He rolled past Hippo, who started to run after him too.

Hippo and Rhino were soon face-to-face.

"So I'm ugly, am I?" Rhino pawed the ground. He shook his horn and got ready to fight.

"Well, you called me fat!" shouted Hippo.

"I did not!" said Rhino. "Hare told me what you said!"

Then Rhino stopped shouting. So did Hippo. They both turned to look at Hare. He ran off laughing.

Since that time Rhino and Hippo have never again been good friends. They only meet at the water hole. And each stays on his own side.

Hare drinks there too. But his real name is Jealousy. And he still whispers to each large animal about the other.

Point of View

A MENDE PEOPLE TALE

Something may seem like a mountain to an ant. But the same thing may seem like a pebble to a giraffe. You see, it is all a matter of your point of view.

This is true for animals. And it is also true for people.

Once two men were going to market. Before they arrived, it got dark.

"Day is ending. The sun is setting," said one man.

"Oh, no," said the other. "Night is beginning. The moon is rising."

The two men began to argue. Which one was right?

They kept arguing while they looked for a place to stay. Soon they found a room for the night. There they got ready for bed.

One man said, "We must sleep at the foot of our beds. That way we will face east when morning comes."

The other man didn't think that was a good idea. "If we do, that end will be the head of the bed."

"You are so stupid!" cried the first man. He pointed to the end of one bed. "Just look! That is the head of this bed." Then he pointed to the other end. "And that is the foot of this bed."

"There is no head. And there is no foot," said the second man. "A head has eyes, a nose, and a mouth. A foot has a heel and toes. A bed has none of these things."

So the men went on arguing. Which man was right?

(If you must know, they both slept on the floor.)

In the middle of the night, one man started to snore. The other man started to walk in his sleep.

The sleepwalker thought he was off on a great trip. Then he tripped over his friend.

The snorer thought he was being chased by a huge elephant. He let out a loud snore.

Both men woke up at the same time.

The sleepwalker was standing over the snorer. The snorer looked up at him.

The snorer still had his mouth open. The sleepwalker looked down at him.

"Your sleepwalking woke me up," said the snorer.

"Your snoring woke me up," said the sleepwalker.

They argued until daylight came.

Then one man said the night was gone because the sun was up. The other said the day had come because the moon had set.

And so they argued some more.

Which man was right?

Does it matter?

Tortoise Cracks His Shell

AN AFRICAN TORTOISE TALE

Don't listen to Tortoise's story about how his shell got cracked. And don't feel sorry for him. It's Tortoise's fault that it happened. And no one else's. Just ask Monkey. He knows the real story.

The bottom of Tortoise's shell was once bright yellow. Everybody said it was the most beautiful thing around. At least that's what Monkey and Buzzard told Tortoise. They were his friends.

Hearing this made Tortoise proud. Much too proud. So Tortoise gave Monkey a job. First Monkey had to wax the bottom of Tortoise's shell with palm oil. Next Monkey would polish the shell with Buzzard's old feathers. And then Monkey would paint Tortoise's toenails with red berry juice.

Tortoise paid Monkey for doing all these things. Monkey also kept Tortoise right side up. He did this for free.

One day Buzzard had an idea. He said that Tortoise should lie on his back. That would give everyone a chance to see his beautiful bright yellow shell. Buzzard told Tortoise, "No one can see the bottom of your shell now. But if you turn over, it will be different. Even the goats on the mountaintops will be able to see it."

Tortoise thought that was a great idea.

Monkey wasn't so sure. "I don't know," he said. "I saw Buzzard licking his lips. You know all he ever thinks about is his next meal. If you turn over on your back, you might dry up. Then you'll die. Next thing you know, Buzzard will be eating you for breakfast. Forget Buzzard. Stick with me, and you can't go wrong."

One day Monkey was hard at work. He was waxing, polishing, and painting Tortoise. "Your shell is as bright as the sun," he said.

Hearing this made Tortoise very happy. "Put a little more palm oil on me," he told Monkey. "Right in the middle where my wide spots are."

Monkey had more to say. "Ah, Tortoise, you are brighter than the sun. You are so bright you could make the plants grow. I bet you could even dry up the lakes."

"Do you really think so?" asked Tortoise. He began to think great thoughts about himself. "Why, I could make the grass grow. I could make water disappear. That would be big stuff!"

Monkey started to sing. And he kept waxing and polishing Tortoise. He sang so long that he used up half a bottle of oil and 15 feathers.

This is what Monkey sang:

You could hang up there in the sky all day.
You could knock that old sun out of the way.
Your shell could shine all day and night.
Your shell could shine so very bright.

All afternoon Tortoise thought about himself and the sun. He decided that Monkey was right. He could take the sun's place. So he looked around. He saw Buzzard sitting in a tree not too far away.

"Buzzard. Do you think my shell is shiny?" he asked.

"I was just thinking about how bright it is," said Buzzard. Buzzard hadn't really been thinking that. He had been listening to his stomach growl. As usual, Buzzard was hungry.

"Is my shell really as bright as the sun?" asked Tortoise.

"Even brighter," said Buzzard.

Tortoise got very excited when he heard that. "So bright that it could grow crops?" he cried. "So bright that it could dry up lakes? That's what Monkey said. He said I should hang in the sky all day. He said I could knock that old sun right out of the sky."

"Well, why not?" said Buzzard. (But Buzzard never believed a word Monkey said.)

"That's it then," said Tortoise. "Buzzard, will you take me up into the sky? I want to start making the crops grow. And making the lakes dry up."

"I'd be happy to," said Buzzard. Of course, he didn't ask Tortoise how he planned to stay in the sky. That wasn't his problem.

So Tortoise slowly climbed up on Buzzard's back. Buzzard lifted his wings and rose into the air. Soon the two animals were flying high in the sky.

Tortoise was excited. He kept thinking about how wonderful it would be to hang in the sky. About what it would be like to rise in the east every morning. And of how surprised the other animals would be to see him.

Tortoise couldn't wait any longer. He waved one foot in the air. "This spot looks good. Just let me off here, Buzzard."

"Okay," said Buzzard. "Here you go." And he shook Tortoise off his back.

Well, Tortoise didn't hang there in the sky. He fell straight to the ground. And when he hit, he bounced three times. Ouch! Ouch! Ouch!

The fall knocked Tortoise out. When he came to, he was glad to find that he was still in one piece. But his shell wasn't. Bits of it were all over the place. Monkey was picking them up and putting them into a basket.

"You and old Baldbrain sure get some great ideas," he said. But Tortoise hurt too much to answer. Later Tortoise paid Monkey to put his shell back together. But Monkey didn't do a very good job.

Now Tortoise doesn't want anyone to look at his cracked shell. And he doesn't want anyone to ask how it got that way. So whenever anyone comes near, Tortoise pulls his head inside his shell and hides.

The Marriage of the Mouse

AN ETHIOPIAN TALE

Once a beautiful white mouse was born. As he grew, he became more and more handsome. His friends and family saw how grand he was. And they saw how his fur was the purest white.

His parents asked themselves, "What will we do? How will we ever find a wife good enough for our son?"

At last the time came for them to find him a wife. They had decided that only God's family was good enough. And that's where they would go to find a wife.

They followed the old customs. That meant that three older mice in the family would visit God. They would ask him for a wife for the handsome young mouse.

The three mice went to stand in front of God's house.

"Why are you standing at the door?" God asked. This meant they could enter. So the mice went in. They said, "We are sent by the family of the beautiful white mouse. We are sure you have heard of him. He is as white as snow. The most beautiful of all creatures. We are looking for a wife for him. Only your family can have a wife good enough. For your family is the greatest and strongest in all the world."

God was quiet for a bit. Then he said, "That is a good thought. It is true that the young mouse should have just the right wife. But I am afraid you have come to the wrong house. For there is a family stronger than mine. It is the family of the Wind."

"That cannot be," the mice said. "You must be stronger than the Wind."

"It might seem that way," said God. "But it is not so. The Wind is stronger than I am. When he blows, he covers the world with dust. He even blows dust in my eyes. So you can see that he is stronger."

The three mice talked together. They agreed that God was right. They needed to go to the Wind. Only his family could have the right wife for the young mouse.

"Where is the house of the Wind?" they asked. God smiled and told them. So they left at once.

When they got to the Wind's house, they stood outside. The Wind asked, "Why are you standing at the door?"

So the mice went inside. "We are looking for a wife for the best mouse of all," they said. "We went to God's house first. But he said the Wind is even stronger than he is. And so we have come to you. We would like a daughter from your family to marry our mouse."

The Wind listened and thought. At last he said, "That is a very good idea. I thank you for it. But I am not the strongest of all. I can blow hard enough to raise the dust and uproot trees. But I am no match for the Mountain. No matter how hard I blow, he does not move. I always have to give up. So you can see that the Mountain is stronger than I am."

"Where does the Mountain live?" asked the three mice.

The Wind told them. So they thanked him and left. When they came to the house of the Mountain, they stood outside.

"Why are you standing at the door?" asked the Mountain.

So they went inside. There the Mountain greeted them in the usual way. "How are you? Did you bring good news? How are your children?"

They answered him. Then they spoke of the beautiful young mouse. They told about how they were looking for a wife.

The Mountain listened carefully. When they were done, he said. "Yes, you are right. Such a creature should have the best wife you can find. But it is not my family that can give him such a wife. There is another who is stronger than I am. He digs at my feet day and night. He makes holes in my sides. He makes me crumble. It is his family that is the strongest."

"Ah, such a creature is truly strong!" said the mice. "Where can we find him?"

The Mountain told them. And they went off again. Soon they reached the spot the Mountain had told them about.

But they were greatly surprised. It was the home of a Mouse.

"Why are you standing at the door?" asked the Mouse.

Once again they went inside. Once again they told their story.

The Mouse listened. Then he said, "You have found a wife for your young mouse! How happy I am that our families can become one!"

And in this way, the beautiful white mouse found a wife. One who was good enough for him.

The Play

The Marriage of the Mouse

AN ETHIOPIAN TALE

Cast of Characters

Storyteller

Mother

Father

First Messenger

Second Messenger

Third Messenger

God

Wind

Mountain

Mouse

Storyteller: Once a beautiful white mouse was born. As he grew, he became more and more handsome. All his friends and family knew this was so.

Mother: How grand our child is. And how handsome.

Father: And how white his fur is. The purest white there is.

Mother: Now it is time to find a wife for our son. What will we do?

Father: How will we ever find a wife good enough for such a mouse?

Mother: There is only one family that will do. We must send messengers to talk to God.

Father: You are right. Only God's family can have a daughter who is good enough.

Storyteller: So the white mouse's mother and father asked three older mice in their family to help. As was the custom, these mice would be their messengers. They would go and find a wife for the young mouse.

First Messenger:	We are here.
Second Messenger:	How can we help you?
Third Messenger:	What can we do?
Father:	It is time to find a wife for our son.
Mother:	And only the best and most beautiful wife will do.
Father:	So we want you to go to God. We want one of his daughters to be our son's wife.
First Messenger:	You are right.
Second Messenger:	Only God's family is good enough.
Third Messenger:	So we will go to his house and talk to him.
Storyteller:	And so the three messengers said good-bye. They headed for God's house. When they got there, they stood outside the door and waited. This was the custom.
God:	Why are you standing at the door?

Storyteller: That question meant that the messengers could go into the house. So they did.

First Messenger: We are sent by the family of the beautiful white mouse. I am sure you have heard of him.

Second Messenger: He is as white as snow. And he is the most beautiful of all creatures.

Third Messenger: Now we are looking for a wife for him. Only your family can have a wife good enough. For your family is the greatest and strongest in all the world.

Storyteller: God was quiet for a bit. He needed some time to think. While he thought, the messengers waited.

God: That is a good thought, my friends. And it is true that the young mouse should have just the right wife.

First Messenger: Then your daughter will be his wife?

God:	Oh, no. I am afraid you have come to the wrong house. For there is a family stronger than mine.
Second Messenger:	How can that be? *Who* can that be?
God:	Why, it is the family of the Wind.
Third Messenger:	That cannot be. You must be stronger than the Wind.
God:	It might seem that way. But it is not so. The wind is stronger than I am. When he blows, he covers the world with dust. He even blows dust in *my* eyes. So you can see that he is stronger.
Storyteller:	Well, the three messengers were very surprised to hear this. They talked together for a moment. And they had to agree. The Wind was stronger than God.
First Messenger:	You are right. We must go and talk to the Wind.

The Play: The Marriage of the Mouse

Second Messenger: Yes. Only his family could have the right wife for our handsome young mouse.

Third Messenger: Can you tell us where to find the house of the Wind?

God: Yes, my friends. I can tell you.

Storyteller: So the three messengers left at once. They walked the way God had sent them. Soon they got to the Wind's house. As was the custom, they stood outside.

Wind: Why are you standing at the door?

First Messenger: We are looking for a wife for the best mouse of all.

Second Messenger: We went to God's house first. But he said you are even stronger than he is.

Third Messenger: And so we have come to you. We would like a daughter from your family to marry our mouse.

Wind: I see. I see. That is a very good idea. I thank you for it. But I am not the strongest of all.

First Messenger:	What?!
Second Messenger:	How can that be?
Third Messenger:	Then who is?
Wind:	I can blow hard enough to raise the dust and uproot trees. But I am no match for the Mountain. No matter how hard I blow, he does not move. I always have to give up. So you can see that the Mountain is stronger than I am.
Storyteller:	So once again, the messengers had to go on their way. This time they went the way the Wind had told them to go. When they came to the house of the Mountain, they stood outside.
Mountain:	Why are you standing at the door? Come in.
First Messenger:	Thank you. We will.
Mountain:	How are you? Did you bring good news? How are your children?
Second Messenger:	All is well with us. We hope it is with you too.

Third Messenger: And we do bring good news. We are looking for a wife for the most beautiful young mouse in the world.

First Messenger: And only your family can have a wife good enough for him.

Mountain: I see. I see. Yes, you are right. Such a wonderful creature should have the best wife you can find. But it is not my family that can give you such a wife.

Second Messenger: How can this be? You are the strongest of all. Even the Wind says so.

Mountain: There is another who is stronger than I am. He digs at my feet day and night. He makes holes in my sides. He makes me crumble. It is his family that is the strongest.

Third Messenger: Ah, such a creature is truly strong! Where can we find him?

Storyteller: So the Mountain told them. And the three mice set off again. Soon they reached the spot the Mountain had told them about. They stopped and stared in surprise.

First Messenger: This can't be right! This is the home of a Mouse!

Mouse: Why are you standing at the door?

Second Messenger: We are looking for a wife for the most beautiful young mouse.

Third Messenger: But his wife must come from the strongest family in the world.

Mouse: And so you have come to me. You are right to do so. At last you have found a wife good enough for your young mouse! I am glad that our families can become one!

Storyteller: And in this way, the beautiful white mouse found a wife. One who was good enough for him.